COYOTE
STEALS THE BLANKET
A Ute Tale

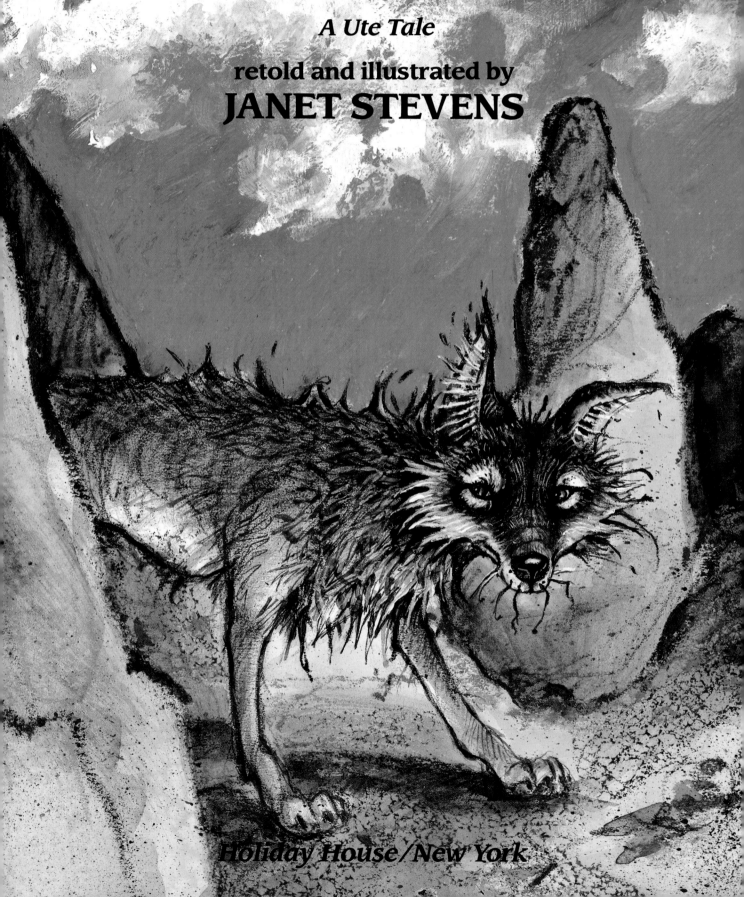

COYOTE
STEALS THE BLANKET

A Ute Tale

retold and illustrated by
JANET STEVENS

Holiday House/New York

For Chris, Dave, Ryan, and Shannon.
"It's a pirate's life for us!"
And thank you, Lindsey, for all your help.

The author gratefully acknowledges the story "Coyote Steals
the Blanket," from *Coyote the Trickster* by Gail Robinson &
Douglas Hill, published by Crane, Russak & Company, Inc. in
1976, which was used as a source for *Coyote Steals the Blanket*
by kind permission of Watson, Little Limited.

Library of Congress Cataloging-in-Publication Data
Stevens, Janet
Coyote steals the blanket : A Ute tale / retold and illustrated
by Janet Stevens.
p.   cm.
Summary: Coyote receives his comeuppance when he tries to take
something that does not belong to him.
ISBN 0-8234-0996-1
1. Ute Indians—Legends.   2. Coyote (Legendary character)
[1. Coyote (Legendary character)   2. Ute Indians—Legends.
3. Indians of North America—Legends.]   I. Title.
E99.U8S795   1993   92-54415   CIP   AC
398.2'089974—dc20
ISBN 0-8234-1129-X (pbk.)

Coyote darted in and out, back and forth among the rocks.

"I go where I want, I do what I want, and I take what I want," he bragged. "I should be crowned King of the Desert."

Just then, Hummingbird zoomed by.

Whirrr! Whirrr! Whirrr!

Coyote's ears twitched. "There's that bird again," he muttered.

"You're going the wrong way," Hummingbird said. "You should take the high road. It's safer."

"Leave me alone," said Coyote. "I go where I want, I do what I want, and I take what I want."

"There is danger ahead," warned Hummingbird.

"Danger?" said Coyote. "I'm not afraid of anything. You can't tell me what to do!"

Coyote turned and ran off.

Hummingbird called after him, "Up ahead there are some beautiful blankets. Whatever you do, *don't* touch them!"

"Why not?" cried Coyote.

"Because they don't belong to you," answered Hummingbird.

"Hummingbird doesn't know what she's talking about," thought Coyote. "How can there be blankets out here in the middle of nowhere?"

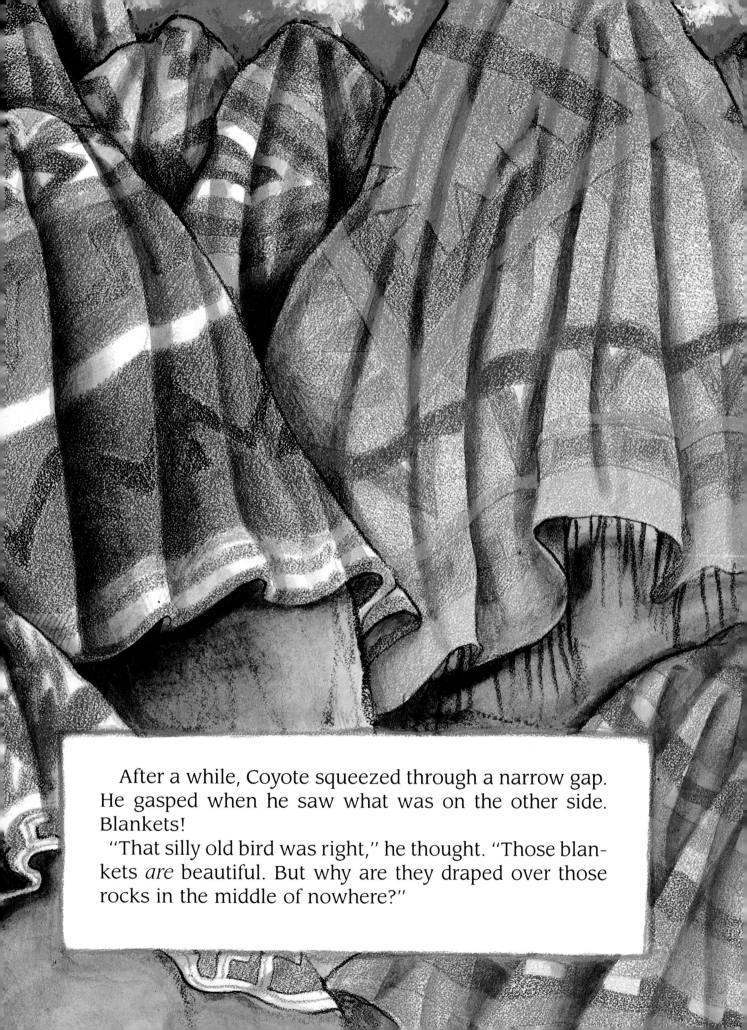

After a while, Coyote squeezed through a narrow gap. He gasped when he saw what was on the other side. Blankets!

"That silly old bird was right," he thought. "Those blankets *are* beautiful. But why are they draped over those rocks in the middle of nowhere?"

Coyote ran over and sniffed one of the blankets.
"I would look fine dressed up in this. I could wear it as a new coat."

"Now, what was it Hummingbird said? That I'm not sup-
posed to touch these blankets? What does she know?"
Coyote put on his fine new coat and dashed away.

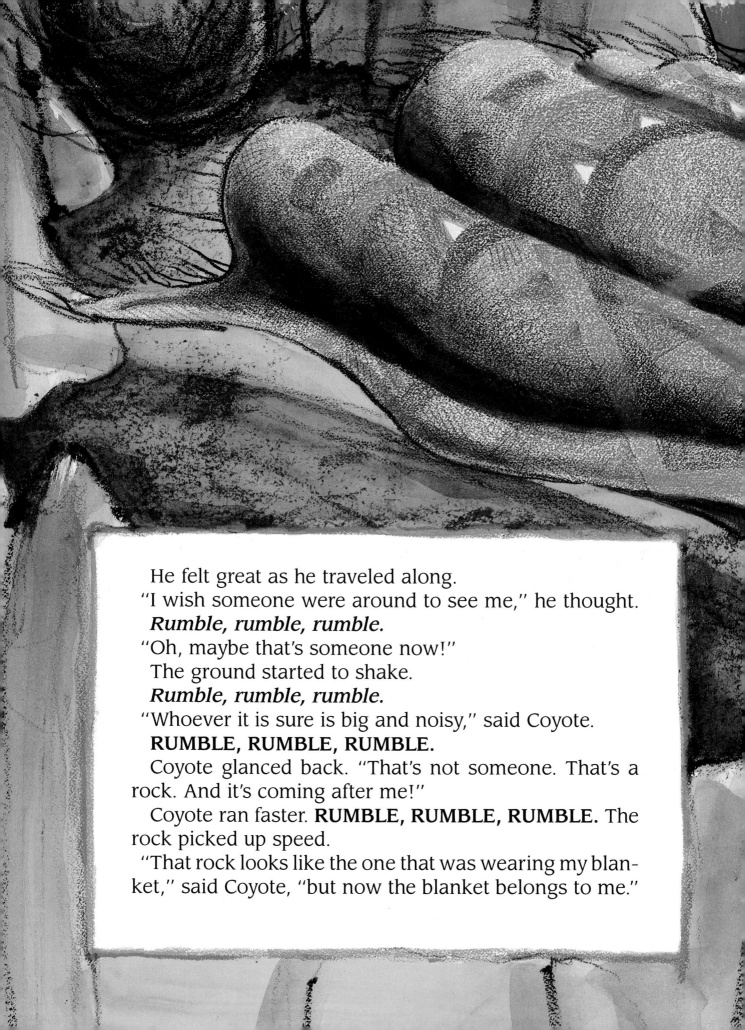

He felt great as he traveled along.

"I wish someone were around to see me," he thought.

Rumble, rumble, rumble.

"Oh, maybe that's someone now!"

The ground started to shake.

Rumble, rumble, rumble.

"Whoever it is sure is big and noisy," said Coyote.

RUMBLE, RUMBLE, RUMBLE.

Coyote glanced back. "That's not someone. That's a rock. And it's coming after me!"

Coyote ran faster. **RUMBLE, RUMBLE, RUMBLE.** The rock picked up speed.

"That rock looks like the one that was wearing my blanket," said Coyote, "but now the blanket belongs to me."

Coyote ran on and on through the canyon. Finally, the rock disappeared.

"No rock in sight," thought Coyote. "I can outrun a rock anyday."

RUMBLE, RUMBLE, RUMBLE.
The rock was back. It was coming around the cliff.

"Oh, no," cried Coyote, and he dashed off.

Each time Coyote stopped and glanced back, the rock was getting closer.

Coyote tried to run faster. He was getting tired.

Finally, exhausted, he collapsed in the middle of the path.

"Surely I'm safe now," he said.

But—**RUMBLE, RUMBLE, RUMBLE**—the rock was still there.

Coyote jumped up and ran off.

Mule Deer was grazing nearby.

"Hey, Mule Deer," Coyote called out. "Can you help me? A killer rock is trying to crush me, and I'm weak from all this running. You're so strong, you could stop that rock with your powerful antlers."

"I *am* strong, Coyote," Mule Deer agreed, puffing out his mighty chest. "I will help you."

RUMBLE, RUMBLE, RUMBLE.
   Mule Deer lowered his giant antlers just as the rock
came crashing toward him.

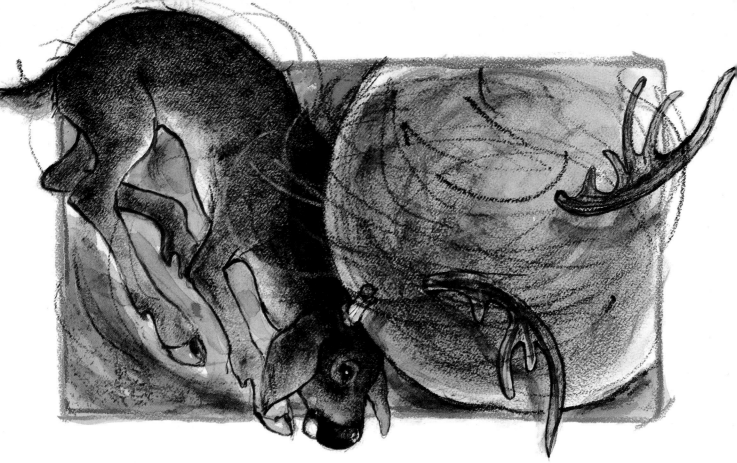

CRACK went the antlers. BOOM went Mule Deer. RUMBLE, RUMBLE, RUMBLE went the rock. It headed straight for Coyote.

Coyote howled and darted away.

He looked back. The rock was dangerously close. **RUMBLE, RUMBLE, RUMBLE.** Coyote's paws ached and his muscles hurt.

"Who does this rock think he is?" he thought. "I am Coyote. GO AWAY!" he screamed. But the rock rolled closer.

Coyote saw Big Horn Sheep resting on the moun- tainside.

"Hey, Sheep," he called out. "Can you help me? A killer rock is trying to crush me, and I'm weak from all this running. You're so strong, you could stop that rock with your powerful legs."

"I *am* strong, Coyote," Big Horn Sheep agreed, puffing out his mighty chest. "I will help you."

Big Horn Sheep lowered his head and kicked his back
legs as the rock came crashing toward him.

CRUNCH went his hooves. **BOOM** went Big Horn Sheep. **RUMBLE, RUMBLE, RUMBLE** went the rock. It headed straight for Coyote.

"Not again!" yelped Coyote and darted away.

It wasn't long before Coyote could go no further.

"Help!" he howled. "Someone save me from the killer rock."

"Give back the blanket," said a tiny voice. Coyote looked up. There was Hummingbird.

"Go away," cried Coyote. "This is my blanket. I will never give it back."

"Then you will be running forever," said Hummingbird.

"I can't run anymore," said Coyote.

"Then you will be crushed," said Hummingbird. "There is a spirit in the rock—the ancient spirit of the great desert. You have taken what does not belong to you. Now you must give it back."

"No!" shouted Coyote.

"Yes!" cried Hummingbird.

"No!"

"Yes!"

"No!"

"Yes!"

RUMBLE, RUMBLE, RUMBLE. There was that rock again.

"Help!" shouted Coyote.

"I should leave you to be crushed," said Hummingbird. "But I can't stand to see an animal hurt, even a coyote."

She whirred her wings with all her might. She created such a tornado that the dust flew, the wind roared . . . and the rock rolled to a stop on Coyote's tail.

Coyote looked over his shoulder. "You stopped the rock, Hummingbird! But now my tail will be as flat as a beaver's."

"THEN GIVE BACK THE BLANKET," said Hummingbird, "and I'll fix your tail."

Coyote pulled and pushed, but he couldn't get the rock to budge. "All right," he said finally. "You win. Here's your old blanket. Now, fix my tail!"

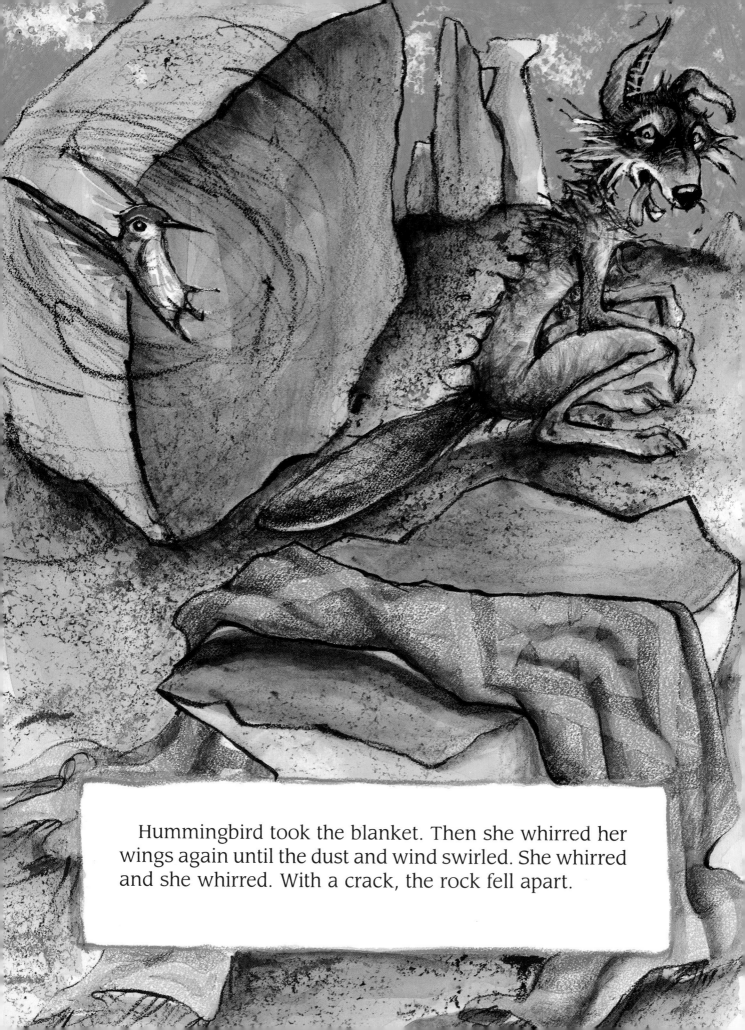

Hummingbird took the blanket. Then she whirred her wings again until the dust and wind swirled. She whirred and she whirred. With a crack, the rock fell apart.

Hummingbird whirred a little more, and Coyote's tail fluffed up.

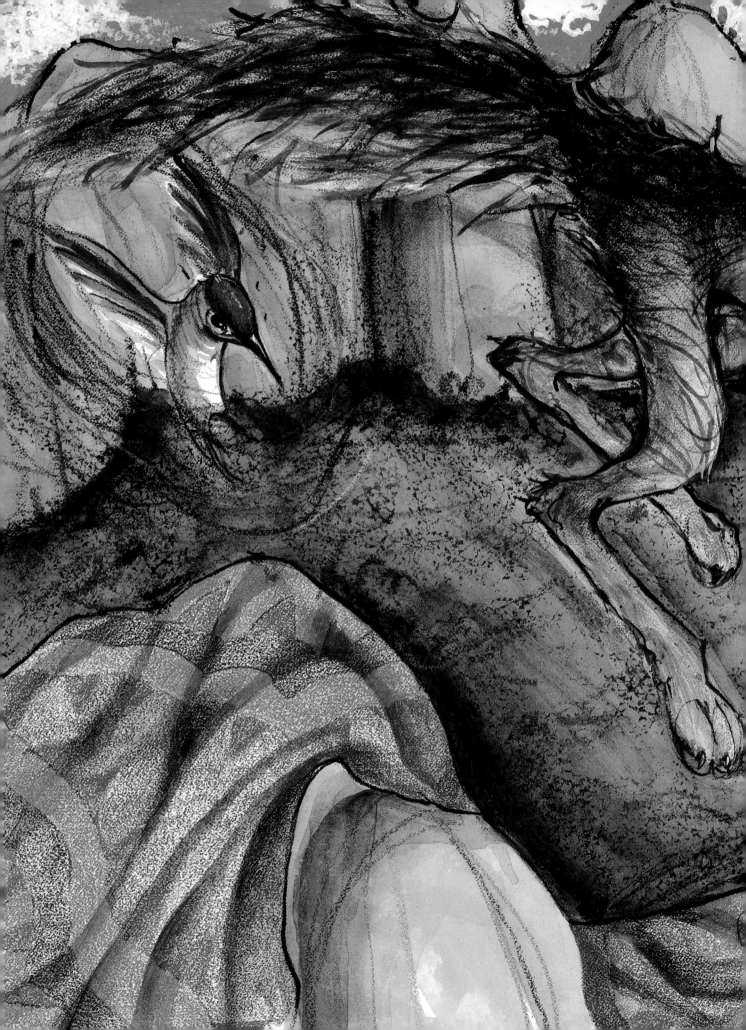

"This place is full of killer rocks and crazy birds," said Coyote. "I'm leaving!"

Coyote dashed off.

Hummingbird shook her head.

"That Coyote," she said. "Will he ever learn?"